THE BOXCAR CHILDREN ®

THE PIZZA MYSTERY

Time to Read® is an early reader program designed to guide children to literacy success regardless of age or grade level. The program's three levels correspond to stages of reading readiness, making book selection straightforward, and assuring that when it's time for a child to read, the right book is waiting.

— Level — 1

Beginning to Read

- Large, simple type
- Basic vocabulary
- Word repetition
- Strong illustration support

— Level — 2

Reading with Help

- Short sentences
- Engaging stories
- Simple dialogue
- Illustration support

— Level — 3

Reading Independently

- Longer sentences
- Harder words
- Short paragraphs
- Increased story complexity

Library of Congress Cataloging-in-Publication data is on file with the publisher.

Copyright © 2021 by Albert Whitman & Company
First published in the United States of America
in 2021 by Albert Whitman & Company
ISBN 978-0-8075-6516-2 (hardcover)
ISBN 978-0-8075-6512-4 (ebook)

THE BOXCAR CHILDREN® is a registered trademark
of Albert Whitman & Company.

TIME TO READ® is a registered trademark
of Albert Whitman & Company.

Printed in China
10 9 8 7 6 5 4 3 2 1 HH 26 25 24 23 22 21

Cover and interior art by Liz Brizzi

Visit The Boxcar Children® online at www.boxcarchildren.com.
For more information about Albert Whitman & Company,
visit our website at www.albertwhitman.com.

THE BOXCAR CHILDREN®

THE PIZZA MYSTERY

Based on the book by
Gertrude Chandler Warner

Albert Whitman & Company
Chicago, Illinois

"I wish our trip wasn't over,"
Violet said.

The Aldens were in Silver Falls.
They were coming home from
their yearly ski trip.

"We aren't done just yet,"
said Grandfather.

"We have one more stop."

"Piccolos' Pizza!" said Benny.

The little pizza place was
Benny's favorite stop on their
winter trips.

Henry, Jessie, Violet, and Benny loved to go on adventures. At one time, the children had lived in a boxcar in the forest. The children had all kinds of adventures in the boxcar.

Then Grandfather found them.
Now they had a real home.
And they still had all kinds of
adventures, as a family.

"I'm going to get the pizza supreme," said Benny. "It's the same every year. And every time it's perfect!"

But something was not the
same about Silver Falls.
The factory in town had grown.
They almost missed the little
pizza shop.

Things had changed inside too.
The booths were empty.
No pizza smell came from
the kitchen.
"Our big pizza oven is broken,"
said Mrs. Piccolo.
"But we can make you a pizza in
our oven upstairs, if you'd like."
Benny nodded.

"Pizza supreme, please!"
But when the pizza came
out, it was not like Benny
remembered.

"What happened here?"
Jessie asked.

Mr. Piccolo sighed.

"The factory has grown.
The owner, Mrs. Sturgis,
is never around.
Now Mr. Irons is in charge.
He doesn't like factory workers
coming over for lunch."

"And our helper, Nick, is sick,"
said Mrs. Piccolo.

"With no help, we may have to
close the shop for good."

The children could not imagine
Silver Falls without Piccolos'.
Violet had an idea.
"Maybe we can stay and help.
Just for a few days."
Grandfather rubbed
his mustache.
The Piccolos were old friends.
"I suppose our trip doesn't
need to end just yet."
The children cheered.

In the apartment upstairs,
the Aldens got to work.
Henry called the gas company
to fix the pizza oven.
Violet made signs for the shop.

Jessie and Benny helped
Mrs. Piccolo make her pizzas.
"Smaller pizzas will cook
better in this small oven,"
Jessie suggested.

The next day, Jessie's pizzas
were a hit.
Customers streamed in.
But no repairman came.
Henry said someone had
canceled the repair.
"Why would they do that?"
asked Violet.
"I don't know," said Henry.
"But we will need that oven
up and running soon."

The repairman came just in
time for the lunch hour.
As he worked, a man came out
from the factory.

It was Mr. Irons, the one filling
in for Mrs. Sturgis.
He let the repairman work.
But he did not look happy.
Had he been the one to cancel
the repair?

With the big oven running, the
Aldens made all kinds of pizzas.
There was one kind Benny
had never tried.
"Zucchini Pizza?" He frowned.
Mrs. Piccolo laughed.
"That was Nick's idea.
I hope he comes back soon.
He's been sick for days."
Benny wasn't so sure about
zucchini on pizza.
But he hoped Nick got better.

Dinner brought an even bigger
crowd to Piccolos' Pizza.
Jessie and Benny baked big
and little pizzas.
Henry served tables.

Violet handed out menus and
half-off coupons she had made.
The smell of pizza filled the
little restaurant.
The future was looking bright.
Until…

The restaurant went dark.

"I'm sorry," said Mr. Piccolo.

"A truck from the factory
hit a power pole, and now the
power is out!"

Dinner ended early.

But that wasn't the only problem.

"If my tomato sauce isn't cold,
it will go bad!" said Mrs. Piccolo.

"And I don't have any fresh
tomatoes to make new sauce."

Jessie had an idea.

She took a snow shovel out
to the garden.

"Are you digging for tomatoes?"
Benny asked.

"Not exactly," said Jessie.

"I'm digging for tomato sauce!"
She placed a jar in the hole.
Then Benny understood.
"The snow will keep it cool!"
Soon the garden was full of jars
of pizza sauce.

The next day, the power
was back.
The sauce was still fresh.
And it was a good thing—
customers flooded in for lunch,
each carrying Violet's coupons.
Henry picked up orders
to deliver by bike.
"That looks like Nick,"
Mr. Piccolo told him.
But when Mr. Piccolo called out,
the man went into the factory.
If Nick was sick, why was he
going to the factory?

At dinner, the biggest crowd yet
came into the pizza shop.
Again, each one held a coupon.
But there was a problem.

"I did not make these,"
said Violet.
"They promise free pizza!"
Someone was trying to hurt
Piccolos' Pizza.

That night, the children talked
about the mystery.
First there was the gas line.
Then the power outage.
Now there were fake coupons.
"That's not all," said Henry.

He told the others about Nick
going into the factory.
Whatever was going on,
it had to do with the factory.
"Maybe we should close down,"
said Mrs. Piccolo.
But Jessie had a better idea.

The next morning, the Aldens
baked the perfect pizza.
One that would make Mr. Irons
change his mind about Piccolos'.
They brought it to the factory,
but in the office wasn't Mr. Irons.
Mrs. Sturgis had returned.

"We think while you were
away someone has been trying
to shut down the pizza shop,"
Jessie said.
"Well, I am back now,"
said Mrs. Sturgis.
"And this pizza is perfect!
Let's get to the bottom of this."

Mr. Irons came into the office. The Aldens went over all the bad things that had happened. "Do you know anything about this?" asked Mrs. Sturgis.

Mr. Irons got angry.

"That building is in the way! If we send the Piccolos packing, we can grow even more!"

Mrs. Sturgis shook her head. "That is no way to do business. I'm afraid you are the one who needs to be sent packing."

The mystery was solved.

Still, Henry had one question.

On the way out, he saw Nick.

"I thought you were sick.

What are you doing here?"

Nick looked worried.

"I come to the factory to eat

lunch with my wife.

When I heard Mr. Irons didn't

want people going to Piccolos',

I called in sick.

I didn't want my wife to get

in trouble."

"That won't be a problem now,"
Mrs. Sturgis assured him.
Still, Nick looked worried.
"I hope the Piccolos will take
me back."

The next day, the Aldens sat
down for one more meal at
Piccolos' Pizza.
The same good smell of pizza
came from the kitchen.
But a new manager delivered it.

Nick placed a big zucchini
pizza on the table.
Benny took a bite and smiled.
Lots of things had changed
at the pizza shop.

But the best parts were still
the same.

Keep reading with the Boxcar Children!

Henry, Jessie, Violet, and Benny used to live in a boxcar. Now they have adventures everywhere they go! Adapted from the beloved chapter book series, these early readers allow kids to begin reading with the stories that started it all.

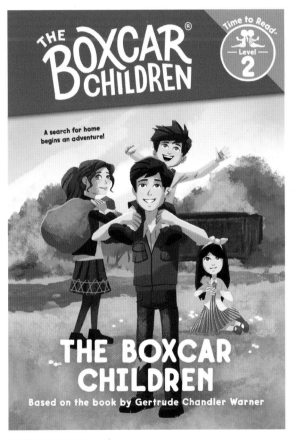

HC 978-0-8075-0839-8 · US $12.99
PB 978-0-8075-0835-0 · US $4.99

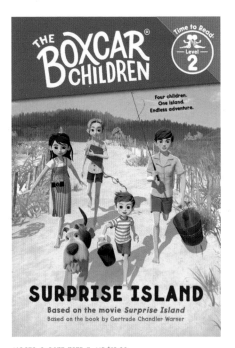

HC 978-0-8075-7675-5 · US $12.99
PB 978-0-8075-7679-3 · US $4.99

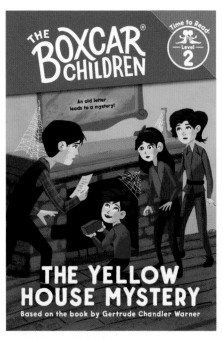

HC 978-0-8075-9367-7 · US $12.99
PB 978-0-8075-9370-7 · US $4.99

HC 978-0-8075-5402-9 · US $12.99
PB 978-0-8075-5435-7 · US $3.99

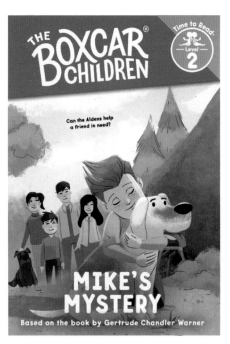

HC 978-0-8075-5142-4 · US $12.99
PB 978-0-8075-5139-4 · US $3.99

HC 978-0-8075-0795-7 · US $12.99
PB 978-0-8075-0800-8 · US $3.99

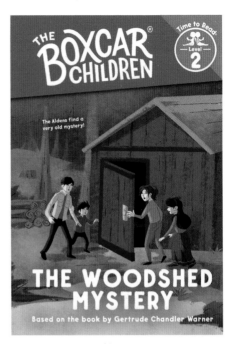

HC 978-0-8075-9210-6 · US $12.99
PB 978-0-8075-9216-8 · US $3.99

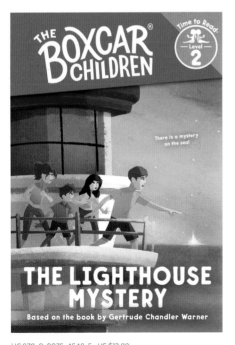

HC 978-0-8075-4548-5 · US $12.99
PB 978-0-8075-4552-2 · US $4.99

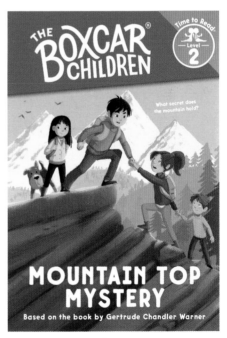

HC 978-0-8075-5291-9 · US $12.99
PB 978-0-8075-5289-6 · US $4.99

GERTRUDE CHANDLER WARNER discovered when she was teaching that many readers who like an exciting story could find no books that were both easy and fun to read. She decided to try to meet this need, and her first book, *The Boxcar Children*, quickly proved she had succeeded.

Miss Warner drew on her own experiences to write the mystery. As a child she spent hours watching trains go by on the tracks opposite her family home. She often dreamed about what it would be like to set up housekeeping in a caboose or freight car—the situation the Alden children find themselves in.

While the mystery element is central to each of Miss Warner's books, she never thought of them as strictly juvenile mysteries. She liked to stress the Aldens' independence and resourcefulness and their solid New England devotion to using up and making do. The Aldens go about most of their adventures with as little adult supervision as possible—something else that delights young readers.

Miss Warner lived in Putnam, Connecticut, until her death in 1979. During her lifetime, she received hundreds of letters from girls and boys telling her how much they liked her books.